Robert Munsch

Illustrated by Michael Martchenko

Up, Up, Down

Scholastic Canada Ltd.

Toronto New York London Auckland Sydney
Mexico City New Delhi Hong Kong Buenos Aires

The illustrations in this book were painted in watercolour on Crescent illustration board.

This book was designed in QuarkXPress,
with type set in 20 point Caslon 224 Medium.

This book has been printed on chlorine-free paper with 10% post-consumer waste.

Canadian Cataloguing in Publicaton Data
Munsch, Robert N., 1945-
Up up down

ISBN 0-439-98815-2

I. Martchenko, Michael. II. Title.

PS8576.U575U6 2001 jC813'.54 C00-932571-9
PZ7.M86Up 2001

ISBN-10 0-439-98815-2 / ISBN-13 978-0-439-98815-5

15 14 13 Printed and bound in Canada 09 10 11

The text has been printed on chlorine-free paper made with 10% post-consumer waste.

To Anna James, Guelph, Ontario
— R.M.

One day Anna, who liked to climb, walked into the kitchen and started to climb up the refrigerator.

She went

up, up, up, up, up, up . . . Fallllll down.

And landed right on her head.

"OW OUCH! OW OUCH! OW OUCH!"

Anna's mother saw her and said,
"Be careful! Don't climb!"

But Anna didn't listen. She went to her bedroom and tried to climb up her dresser.

She went

up, up, up, up, up, up . . . Falllll down.

And landed right on her tummy.

"OW OUCH! OW OUCH! OW OUCH!"

Her father found her on the floor and said, "Be careful! Don't climb."

So Anna decided to go outside where it was okay to climb, and the biggest thing she could find to climb was . . .

The Tree.

Anna went

up, up, up, up, up, up . . . **Fallllll** down.

And landed right on her bottom.

"OW OUCH! OW OUCH! OW OUCH!"

But the next time she was very careful.
She went

up, up, up, up, up, up . . .

all the way to the top of the tree.

And then Anna yelled,
"I'm the king of the castle,
Mommy's a dirty rascal!"

Anna's mother came out of the house
and looked all around. She said,
"Anna? Anna? Anna?

ANNA!
Get out of that **tree!**"

And Anna said, "No, no, no, no, no!"

So her mother tried to climb the tree.
She went

up, up, up, up, up, up . . . Fallllll down.

And landed right on her head.

"OW OUCH! OW OUCH! OW OUCH!"

And then Anna yelled, “I’m the king of the castle, Daddy’s a dirty rascal!”

Anna’s father came out of the house and looked all around.

He said, “Anna? Anna? Anna?

ANNA!

Get out of that **tree**!”

And Anna said, “No, no, no, no, no!”

So her father tried to climb the tree.
He went

up, up, up, up, up, up . . . Fallllll down.

And landed right on his bottom.

"OW OUCH! OW OUCH! OW OUCH!"

Anna leaned over the side of the tree. She looked at her mother and she looked at her father. Her mother was holding her head and yelling,

"WAHHHHH!"

And her father was holding his bottom and yelling,

"OW OW OW OW OW!"

Then Anna climbed

down, down, down, down, down, down,

all the way to the bottom of the tree. She got her brother and sisters, and they ran inside and got ten enormous Band-Aids.

Anna walked over to her mother, took the paper off one Band-Aid:

SCRITCH!

And wrapped it around her mother's head:

WRAP WRAP WRAP WRAP WRAP

Then Anna walked over to her father, took the paper off the other Band-Aid:

SCRITCH!

And wrapped it around her father's bottom:

WRAP WRAP WRAP WRAP WRAP

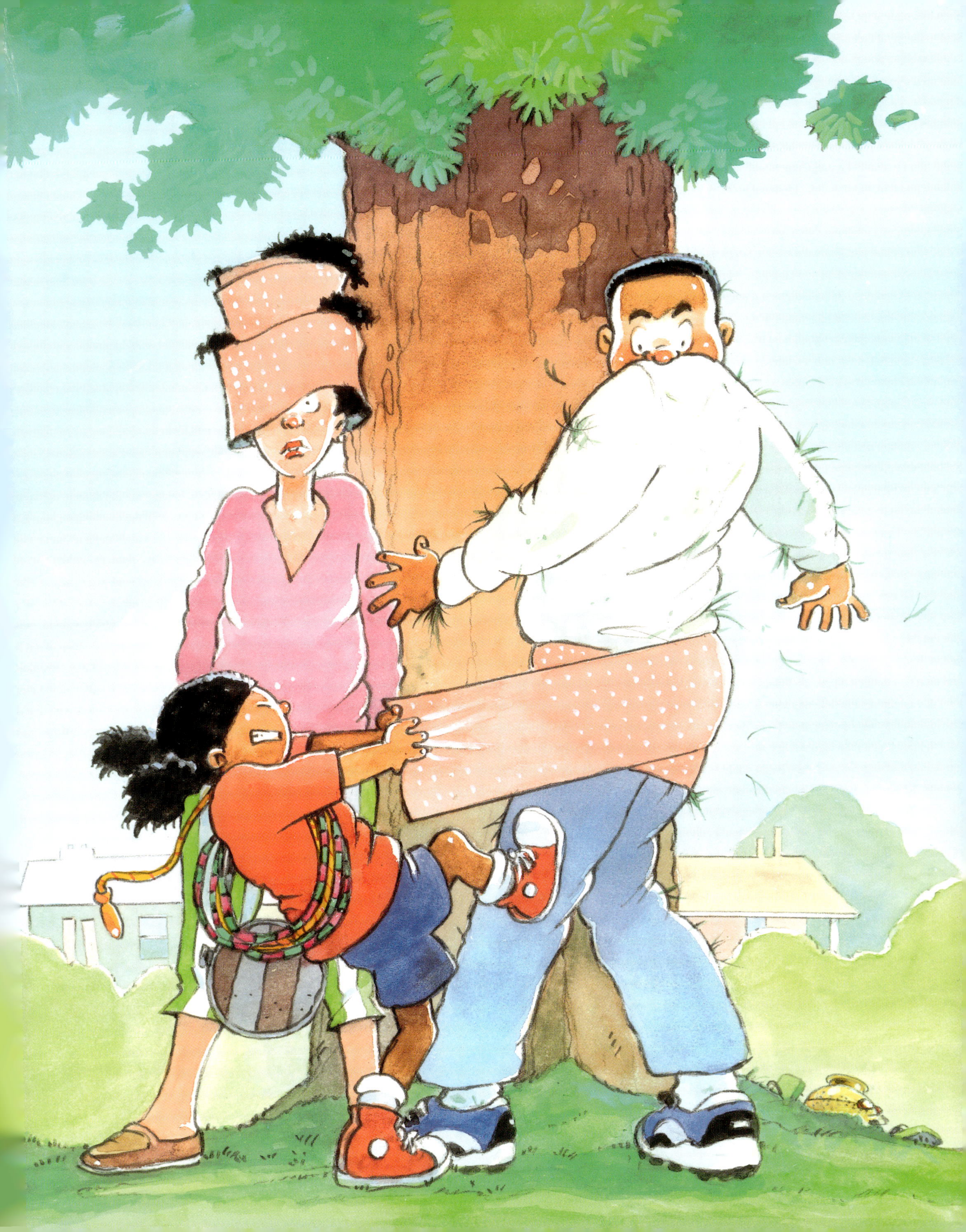

Then Anna looked at her mother and she looked at her father and she said,

"Be CAREFUL — don't CLIMB!"